The Sword in the Bone

Written by
Jonny Zucker

Illustrated by
Beccy Blake

Artie was a puppy that had bags of energy. He loved nothing more than running around all day, catching balls and chasing rabbits. He also loved mess. In fact, his mum's favourite saying was: "Artie. Don't leave your muddy paw prints all over the house – again!"

One morning, after climbing trees at the top of the mountain, Artie ran back home to Dogtown. As soon as he arrived, he noticed that all of the other dogs seemed very quiet and sad.

"What's the matter?" asked Artie. "Everyone looks like they've just lost their favourite ball."

"King Barkalot the Gruff has died," said Artie's older brother Karl, "and, as he has no sons and daughters, no one knows who will be the next king."

"I could do it!" cried Artie. "I could sit on a throne, eat delicious food all day and order everyone around!"

"I'm sorry," said Karl, "but you're not big enough or brave enough to be king. A king is always somebody really special."

Artie felt hurt by his brother's words, so he grabbed his favourite ball and slunk back up the mountain to practise his chasing and fetching skills.

While Artie was away chasing and fetching, the old dog wizard, Melvin, arrived in Dogtown. He stood in the town square, before all the town's dogs.

"I have discovered a way to choose the next king or queen of Dogland," he announced.

"Tell us, O wise Melvin!" shouted Karl, along with all the other dogs.

"In the middle of the forest there is a giant bone," said Melvin. "Fixed into this bone is a gleaming silver sword. Whichever dog can pull that sword out of that bone will be the next king or queen!"

The dogs looked at each other for a moment, then they all turned and started racing towards the forest.

"I'll be the one who can grab that sword!" shouted a small Pekinese dog. "I shall be king of Dogland!"

"No, it'll be me!" shouted a large black labrador.

"Get out of the way, you two!" shouted a bad-tempered bulldog. "That sword is mine. I'll prove it to you!"

A short while later, all the dogs reached the centre of the forest. Everyone skidded to a halt.

Before them stood a large silver sword, glinting in the bright sunlight. The lower half of the sword was buried in a huge, gleaming white bone. On the upper half of the sword, finely written on the blade, were the words:

WHOEVER SHALL PULL ME OUT OF THIS BONE
YE SHALL BE RULER OF THIS WHOLE LAND.

How all those dogs tried to pull, yank and prise the sword out of that bone. How they gripped and growled and groaned. How they sweated and strained and struggled. But, however strong they were, however big their muscles, not one of them could move that sword even a fraction of a millimetre.

After hours of taking it in turns to try to remove the sword from the bone, the forest was full of frustrated and none-too-happy dogs.

With all of their excitement gone, and exhausted by their efforts, they trudged back home, silent and disappointed.

When Artie got back from his chasing and fetching practice, he found everyone sitting around looking miserable.

They must still all be sad about King Barkalot, he thought to himself. *I won't bother them.*

So Artie knew nothing about the special sword in the special bone.

*****

That afternoon, Melvin appeared in Dogtown again. "I have decided to hold a contest," he declared. "We will find out who is the STRONGEST dog in

our town – and he or she will be king or queen."

"Yay!" cried Artie, doing some high kicks and showing off his muddy paws. "That sounds like fun. I could be the next king!"

"Sadly, this contest is not for you," said Karl, putting a paw round his brother's shoulders. "You are too small and weak to join in."

Artie was hurt again, but he cheered up when Karl said he could carry Karl's fighting outfit and paw boxing gloves.

A short while later, everyone was gathered in the town square. "It is time for all participating dogs to get ready," announced Melvin. "The contest will start in twenty minutes."

Karl had already started changing into his fighting outfit when a look of shock spread across his face.

"Oh no!" he howled. "I've left my sword at home."

"Don't worry," said Artie. "I'll race back and get it for you."

"Thanks," nodded Karl, "You may not be anywhere near as strong as me, but you *are* a fast runner."

So Artie turned and sped off.

When he got home though, he couldn't find Karl's sword anywhere. He looked in the cupboards and he looked under the sofa; he even looked under the bed in Karl's very messy bedroom.

But there was no sign of Karl's sword anywhere.

Drat, thought Artie. *Karl won't be very pleased when I show up without his sword.*

Artie started running back to the town square, trying to work out what he could say to Karl. As he ran through forest, he saw something glinting between the trees, in the sunlight.

I wonder what that is, he thought.

Weaving through the trees, Artie came upon a huge white bone. A sparkling silver sword was wedged inside it.

If I can't get Karl his own sword, this one will have to do, thought Artie.

He grabbed the hilt of the sword and gently pulled. It slipped out of the bone as if the bone was made of warm butter.

Without looking at the writing on its blade, Artie started running back through the forest.

When Artie finally reached the town square he was waving the sword in the air, shouting "Karl! Karl! I have a sword for you!" To his astonishment, every dog in the square turned to Artie and bowed its head to him.

"What's the matter?" Artie shouted in shock. "Have you all lost *both* of your favourite balls?"

"No," replied Karl, looking up. "I was wrong about you. *You* are the dog who pulled the sword out of the bone, while all of us failed. *You* are the one."

"Indeed," smiled Melvin. "As the only one with the magical powers to grab that sword, you are the new ruler of this whole land, *King* Artie."

RULER OF THE WHOLE LAND!

Artie couldn't believe it. His whole life was about to change. He was the KING! He'd get to sit on a throne, eat delicious food all day and order everyone around! He could even get a new favourite ball.

However, one thing didn't change.

"Just because you're king now Artie, doesn't mean you can leave muddy paw prints all over the house," said his mum.